This Little Tiger book belongs to:

_____

_____

_____

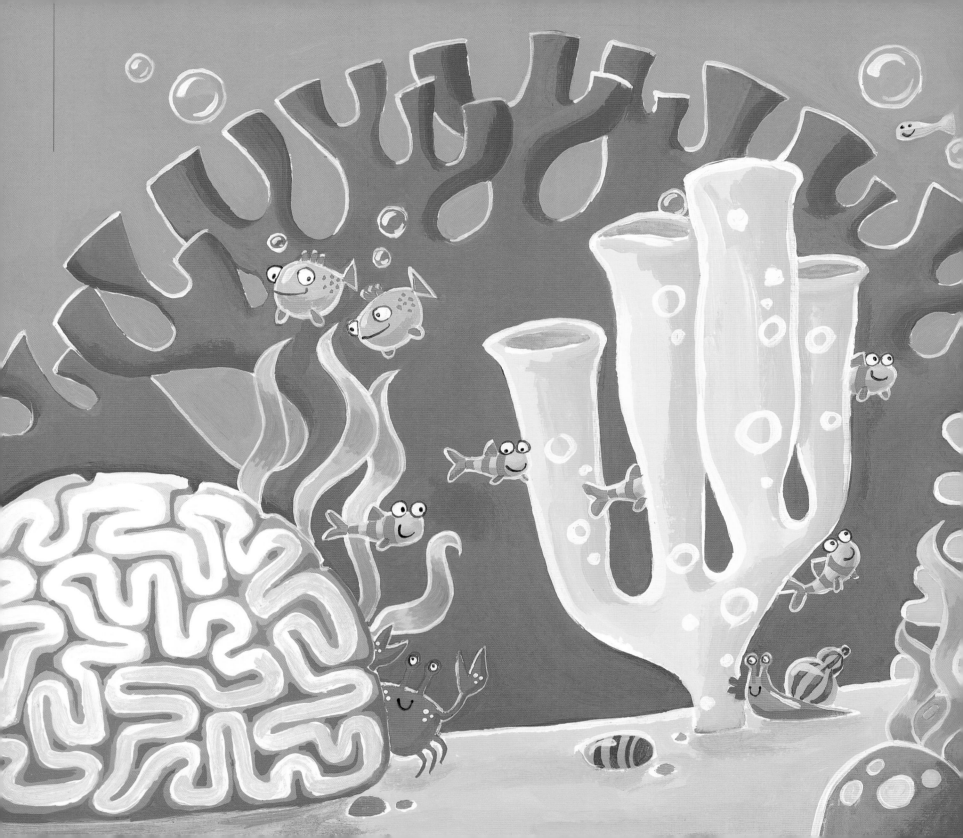

To Wayne, with love

LITTLE TIGER PRESS
An imprint of Magi Publications
1 The Coda Centre, 189 Munster Road,
London SW6 6AW
www.littletigerpress.com

First published in Great Britain 2003
This edition published 2008

Text and illustrations copyright © Ruth Galloway 2003
Ruth Galloway has asserted her right to be
identified as the author and illustrator of this work
under the Copyright, Designs and Patents Act, 1988.

All rights reserved • ISBN 978-1-84506-932-2
Printed in China

2 4 6 8 10 9 7 5 3 1

Smiley Shark

by Ruth Galloway

Far away, in a deep rolling ocean, lived Smiley Shark—
the smiliest and sunniest, the friendliest and funniest,
the biggest and toothiest of all the fish.

Every day Smiley Shark watched the beautiful fish
that dipped and dived, and jiggled and jived,
and darted and dashed with a splish and a splash.

Smiley Shark longed to splish and splash with the other fish. But whenever he smiled at them they swam away.

Smiley Shark swam up to Angelfish.

"Will you play with me?" he asked.

Angelfish shivered and shook, then . . .

SWOOSH!

She raced
away as fast
as she could.

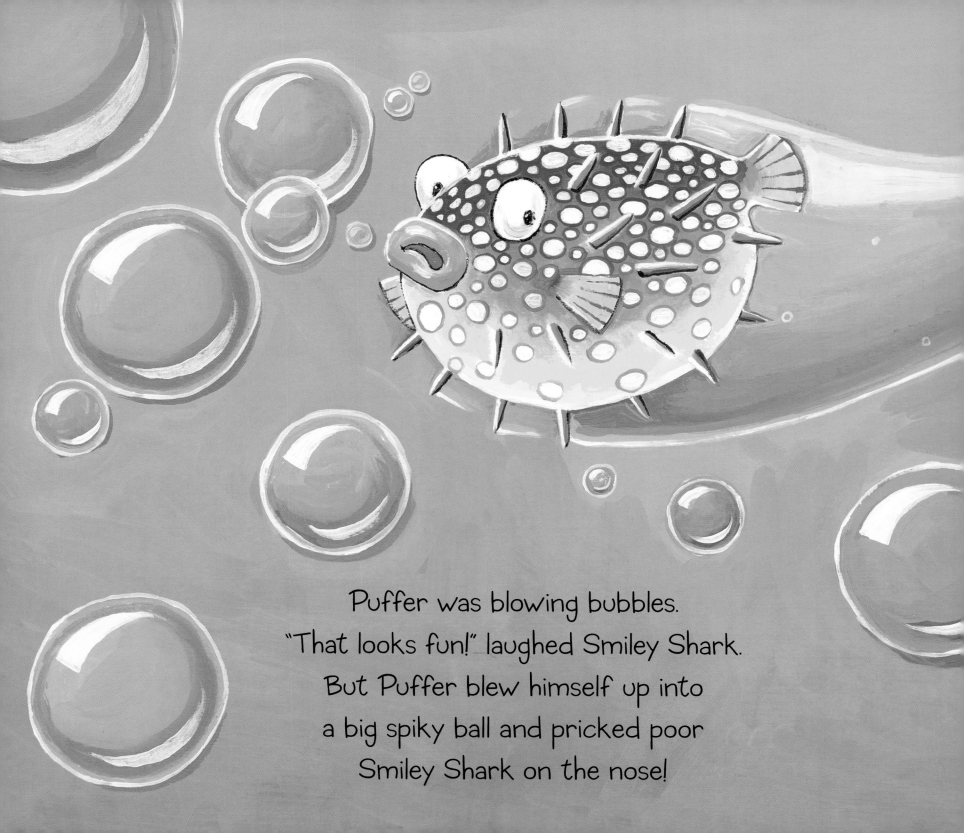

Puffer was blowing bubbles.
"That looks fun!" laughed Smiley Shark.
But Puffer blew himself up into
a big spiky ball and pricked poor
Smiley Shark on the nose!

Starfish was twirling and whirling,
dancing and prancing.
"What fun!" giggled Smiley Shark.
But . . .

SWIRL!

Starfish
twirled off
across the ocean floor.

Smiley Shark showed his
toothy smile to Jellyfish . . .

and Octopus . . .

and Catfish.

In a flash, they all took off
as fast as they could swim.

"Everyone is scared of my big white teeth," wailed Smiley Shark. He didn't feel much like smiling anymore.

SPLiSH! SPLASH!

Twisting and turning, splashing and churning,
the fish danced faster than ever. Smiley Shark
watched from a distance. But this time something
was very wrong. All the fish were . . .

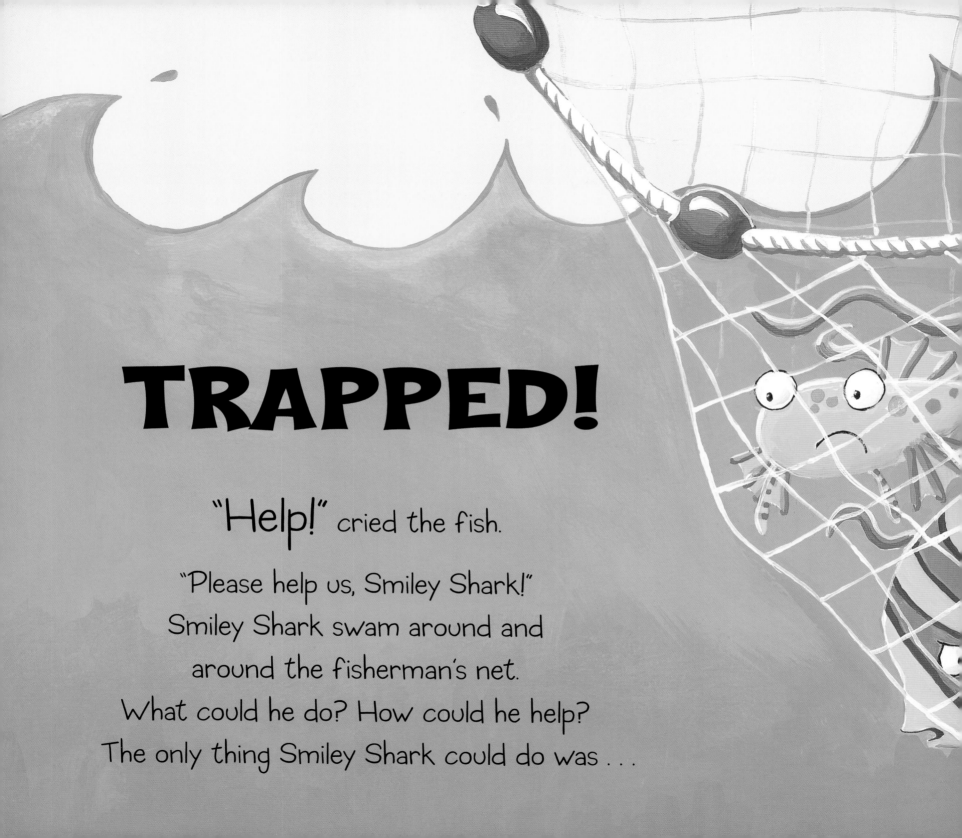

TRAPPED!

"Help!" cried the fish.

"Please help us, Smiley Shark!"
Smiley Shark swam around and
around the fisherman's net.
What could he do? How could he help?
The only thing Smiley Shark could do was . . .

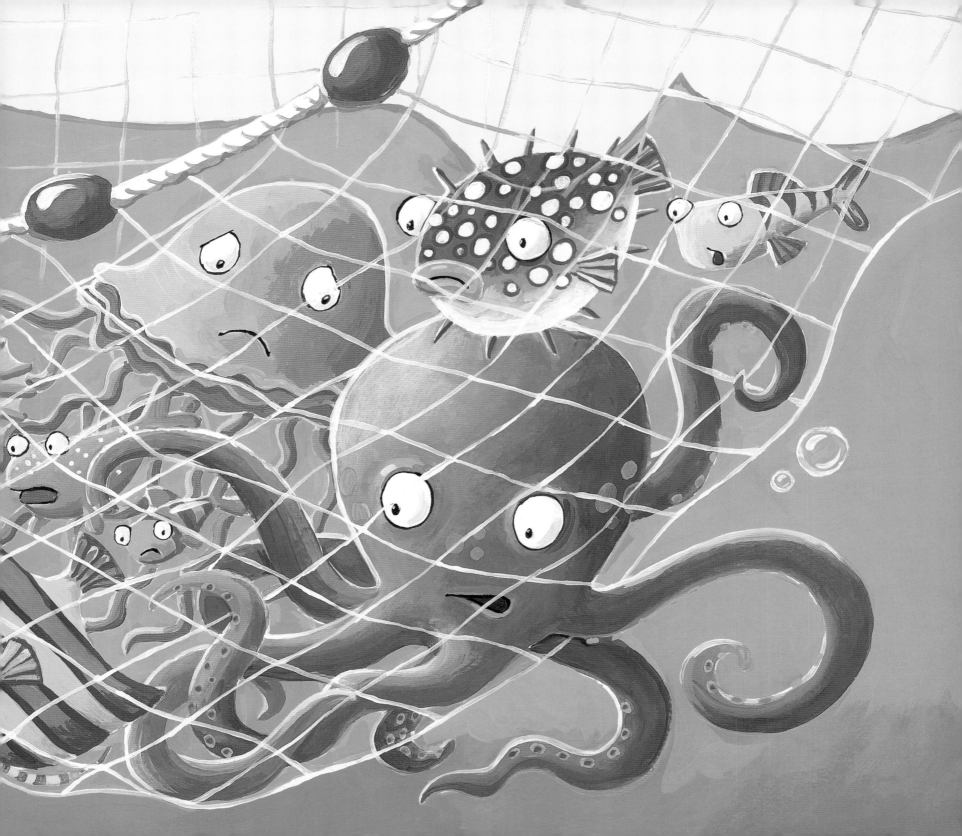

SMILE!

"Aaaaaaaahhhh!" screamed the fisherman, dropping his heavy net into the waves. "I'm getting out of here!" he cried.

"Hurray!" cheered the fish.
"We're safe! Thank you, Smiley Shark!"

Now far away, in the deep rolling ocean, live Smiley Shark and all his friends! And every day they can be seen, dipping and diving, darting and dashing, splishing and splashing and . . .

SMILING!

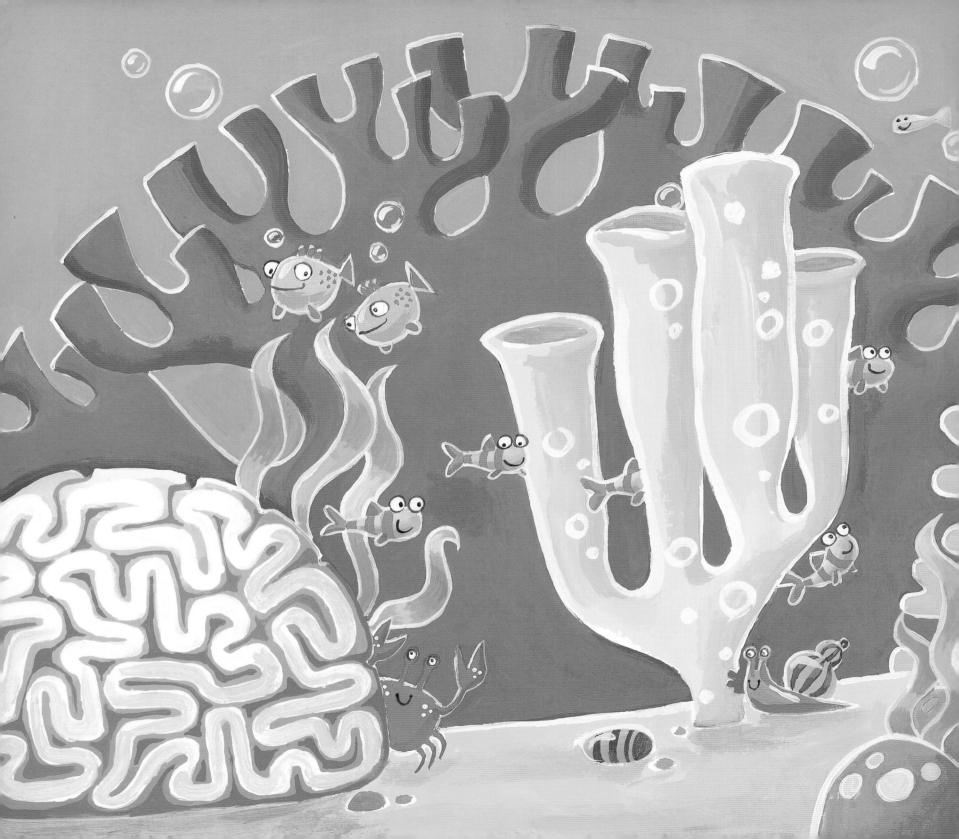